CHRISTMAS TRUCE

Story by
Aaron Shepard

Pictures by
Wendy Edelson

Skyhook Press
Bellingham, Washington

CHRISTMAS TRUCE

Christmas Day, 1914

My dear sister Janet,

It is 2:00 in the morning and most of our men are asleep in their dugouts—yet I could not sleep myself before writing to you of the wonderful events of Christmas Eve. In truth, what happened seems almost like a fairy tale, and if I hadn't been through it myself, I would scarce believe it. Just imagine: While you and the family sang carols before the fire there in London, I did the same with enemy soldiers here on the battlefields of France!

As I wrote before, there has been little serious fighting of late. The first battles of the war left so many dead that both sides have held back until replacements could come from home. So, we have mostly stayed in our trenches and waited.

But what a terrible waiting it has been! Knowing that any moment an artillery shell might land and explode beside us in the trench, killing or maiming several men. And in daylight not daring to lift our heads above ground, for fear of a sniper's bullet.

And the rain—it has fallen almost daily. Of course, it collects right in our trenches, where we must bail it out with pots and pans. And with the rain has come mud—a good foot or more deep. It splatters and cakes everything, and constantly sucks at our boots. One new recruit got his feet stuck in it, and then his hands too when he tried to get out—just like in that American story of the tar baby!

Through all this, we couldn't help feeling curious about the German soldiers across the way. After all, they faced the same dangers we did, and slogged about in the same muck. What's more, their first trench was only fifty yards from ours. Between us lay No Man's Land, bordered on both sides by barbed wire—yet they were close enough we sometimes heard their voices.

Of course, we hated them when they killed our friends. But other times, we joked about them and almost felt we had something in common. And now it seems they felt the same.

Just yesterday morning—Christmas Eve Day—we had our first good freeze. Cold as we were, we welcomed it, because at least the mud froze solid. Everything was tinged white with frost, while a bright sun shone over all. Perfect Christmas weather.

During the day, there was little shelling or rifle fire from either side. And as darkness fell on our Christmas Eve, the shooting stopped entirely. Our first complete silence in months! We hoped it might promise a peaceful holiday, but we didn't count on it. We'd been told the Germans might attack and try to catch us off guard.

I went to the dugout to rest, and lying on my cot, I must have drifted asleep. All at once my friend John was shaking me awake, saying, "Come and see! See what the Germans are doing!" I grabbed my rifle, stumbled out into the trench, and stuck my head cautiously above the sandbags.

I never hope to see a stranger and more lovely sight. Clusters of tiny lights were shining all along the German line, left and right as far as the eye could see.

"What is it?" I asked in bewilderment, and John answered, "Christmas trees!"

And so it was. The Germans had placed Christmas trees in front of their trenches, lit by candle or lantern like beacons of good will.

And then we heard their voices raised in song.

Stille nacht, heilige nacht . . .

This carol may not yet be familiar to us in Britain, but John knew it and translated: "Silent night, holy night." I've never heard one lovelier—or more meaningful, in that quiet, clear night, its dark softened by a first-quarter moon.

When the song finished, the men in our trenches applauded. Yes, British soldiers applauding Germans! Then one of our own men started singing, and we all joined in.

The first Nowell, the angel did say . . .

In truth, we sounded not nearly as good as the Germans, with their fine harmonies. But they responded with enthusiastic applause of their own and then began another.

O Tannenbaum, o Tannenbaum . . .

Then we replied.

O come all ye faithful . . .

But this time they joined in, singing the words in Latin.

Adeste fideles . . .

British and German harmonizing across No Man's Land! I would have thought nothing could be more amazing—but what came next was more so.

"English, come over!" we heard one of them shout. "You no shoot, we no shoot."

There in the trenches, we looked at each other in bewilderment. Then one of us shouted jokingly, "You come over here."

To our astonishment, we saw two figures rise from the trench, climb over their barbed wire, and advance unprotected across No Man's Land. One of them called, "Send officer to talk."

I saw one of our men lift his rifle to the ready, and no doubt others did the same—but our captain called out, "Hold your fire." Then he climbed out and went to meet the Germans halfway. We heard them talking, and a few minutes later, the captain came back with a German cigar in his mouth!

"We've agreed there will be no shooting before midnight tomorrow," he announced. "But sentries are to remain on duty, and the rest of you, stay alert."

Across the way, we could make out groups of two or three men starting out of trenches and coming toward us. Then some of us were climbing out too, and in minutes more, there we were in No Man's Land, over a hundred soldiers and officers of each side, shaking hands with men we'd been trying to kill just hours earlier!

Before long a bonfire was built, and around it we mingled—British khaki and German grey. I must say, the Germans were the better dressed, with fresh uniforms for the holiday.

Only a couple of our men knew German, but more of the Germans knew English. I asked one of them why that was.

"Because many have worked in England!" he said. "Before all this, I was a waiter at the Hotel Cecil. Perhaps I waited on your table!"

"Perhaps you did!" I said, laughing.

He told me he had a girlfriend in London and that the war had interrupted their plans for marriage. I said, "Don't worry. We'll have you beat by Easter, then you can come back and marry the girl."

He laughed at that. Then he asked if I'd send her a postcard he'd give me later, and I promised I would.

Another German had been a porter at Victoria Station. He showed me a picture of his family back in Munich. His eldest sister was so lovely, I told him I should like to meet her someday. He beamed and said he would like that very much and gave me his family's address.

Even those who could not converse could still exchange gifts— our cigarettes for their cigars, our tea for their coffee, our corned beef for their sausage. Badges and buttons from uniforms changed owners, and one of our lads walked off with the infamous spiked helmet! I myself traded a jackknife for a leather equipment belt—a fine souvenir to show when I get home.

Newspapers too changed hands, and the Germans howled with laughter at ours. They assured us that France was finished and Russia nearly beaten too. We told them that was nonsense, and one of them said, "Well, you believe your newspapers and we'll believe ours."

Clearly they are lied to—yet after meeting these men, I wonder how truthful our own newspapers have been. These are not the "savage barbarians" we've read so much about. They are men with homes and families, hopes and fears, principles and, yes, love of country. In other words, men like ourselves. Why are we led to believe otherwise?

As it grew late, a few more songs were traded around the fire, and then all joined in for—I am not lying to you—"Auld Lang Syne." Then we parted with promises to meet again tomorrow, and even some talk of a football match.

I was just starting back to the trenches when an older German clutched my arm. "My God," he said, "why cannot we have peace and all go home?"

I told him gently, "That you must ask your emperor."

He looked at me then, searchingly. "Perhaps, my friend. But also we must ask our hearts."

And so, dear sister, tell me, has there ever been such a Christmas Eve in all history? And what does it all mean, this impossible befriending of enemies?

For the fighting here, of course, it means regrettably little. Decent fellows those soldiers may be, but they follow orders and we do the same. Besides, we are here to stop their army and send it home, and never could we shirk that duty.

Still, one cannot help imagine what would happen if the spirit shown here were caught by the nations of the world. Of course, disputes must always arise. But what if our leaders were to offer well wishes in place of warnings? Songs in place of slurs? Presents in place of reprisals? Would not all war end at once?

All nations say they want peace. Yet on this Christmas morning, I wonder if we want it quite enough.

Your loving brother,
Tom

ABOUT THE CHRISTMAS TRUCE

The Christmas Truce of 1914 is one of the most extraordinary incidents not only of World War I but of all military history. Providing inspiration for songs, books, plays, and movies, it has endured as an archetypal image of peace.

Starting in some places on Christmas Eve and in others on Christmas Day, the truce covered as much as two-thirds of the British-German front, with French and Belgians involved as well. Thousands of soldiers took part. In most places, it lasted at least through Boxing Day (December 26), and in some, through mid-January. Perhaps most remarkably, it grew out of no single initiative but sprang up in each place spontaneously and independently.

Unofficial and spotty as the truce was, there have been those convinced it never happened—that the whole thing was made up. Others have believed it happened but that the news was suppressed. Neither is true. Though little was publicly reported in Germany, the truce made headlines for weeks in British newspapers, with published letters and photos from soldiers at the front. In a single issue, the latest inflammatory rumor of German atrocities might share space with a photo of British and German soldiers crowded together, their caps and helmets exchanged, smiling for the camera.

Historians, on the other hand, have not shown much interest in an unofficial outbreak of peace. The first comprehensive look at the event came only with the 1981 BBC documentary *Peace in No Man's Land*, by Malcolm Brown and Shirley Seaton, and their 1984 companion book, *Christmas Truce* (Secker & Warburg, London). The book featured a large number of firsthand accounts from letters and diaries. Nearly everything described in my fictional letter is drawn from these accounts—though I have heightened the drama somewhat by selecting, arranging, and compressing.

In my letter, I've tried to counteract two popular misconceptions of the truce. One is that only common soldiers took part in it, while officers opposed it. (Actually, few officers opposed it, and many took part.) The other is that neither side wished to return to fighting. (Most soldiers, especially British, French, and Belgian, remained determined to fight and win.)

Sadly, I also had to omit the Christmas Day games of football— or soccer, as called in the United States—that are often falsely associated with the truce. The truth is that the terrain of No Man's Land ruled out formal games—though certainly some soldiers kicked around balls and makeshift substitutes.

Another false idea about the truce was held even by most soldiers who were there: that it was unique in history. Though the Christmas Truce is the foremost incident of its kind, informal truces were a long-standing military tradition. During the American Civil War, for instance, Rebels and Yankees traded tobacco, coffee, and newspapers, fished peaceably on opposite sides of a stream, and even gathered blackberries together. Some degree of fellow feeling had always been common among soldiers sent to battle.

Of course, all that has changed in modern times. Today, combatants kill at great distances, often with the push of a button and a sighting on a computer screen. Even where soldiers come face to face, their languages and cultures are often so divergent as to make friendly communication unlikely.

No, we should not expect to see another Christmas Truce. Yet still what happened on that Christmas of 1914 may inspire the peacemakers of today—for, now as always, the best time to make peace is long before the armies go to war.

Aaron Shepard

ABOUT THE AUTHOR

Aaron Shepard is the award-winning author of *The Baker's Dozen*, *The Legend of Lightning Larry*, *The Sea King's Daughter*, and many more children's books. Once a professional storyteller, Aaron specializes in lively retellings of folktales and other traditional literature, which have won him honors from the American Library Association, the New York Public Library, the Bank Street College of Education, the National Council for the Social Studies, and the American Folklore Society. Visit him at www.aaronshep.com.

ABOUT THE ILLUSTRATOR

Wendy Edelson is the award-winning illustrator of *The Baker's Dozen*, *The Mice Before Christmas*, *Quackling*, and many more children's books. She has applied her talent to a wide range of illustration projects, including picture books, pet portraits, posters, and puzzles. Among her clients have been Seattle's Woodland Park Zoo, the Seattle Aquarium, Pacific Northwest Ballet, the U.S. Postal Service, *Cricket Magazine*, McGraw-Hill Education, and the American Library Association. Visit her at www.wendyedelson.com.

Also from Skyhook Press . . .

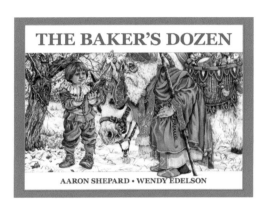

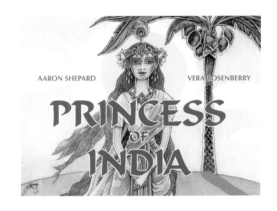

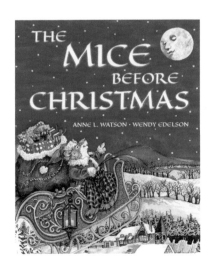

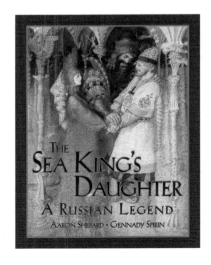

CPSIA information can be obtained
at www.ICGtesting.com
Printed in the USA
BVHW022139171021
618860BV00005B/4